Look and Find®

P9-DFZ-738

Disney

Vampirina

we make books come alive™

pi kids

Phoenix International Publications, Inc.

Chicago • London • New York • Hamburg • Mexico City • Paris • Sydney

Vampirina Hauntley ("Vee" for short!) and her family have just moved from TRANSYLVANIA to Pennsylvania. They have lots of GHOULISH goodies to unpack! Can you find these household items?

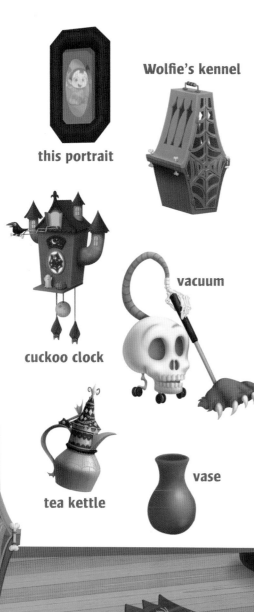

this portrait

Wolfie's kennel

cuckoo clock

vacuum

tea kettle

vase

All the neighbors have come to check out the Hauntleys' new *home*, *SCREAM*, *home*! Look for Vampirina's family, along with some old and new friends:

Vampirina

Boris & Oxana

Poppy

Wolfie

Gregoria

Edgar

Vee is nervous for her first day of school. She feels like she has SPIDERS in her stomach! But with Poppy by her side, and a spooky gift for her new teacher, Vee plans to put her BATTIEST foot forward.

Can you spot these brand-new backpacks?

School takes some getting used to. Vee zooms to the front of the room to introduce herself—and then remembers she can't use her vampire powers around humans!

While Vee adjusts, find these classroom things:

this pencil cup

paint tray

eraser

paint jar

ruler

this book

Each of Mr. Gore's students has a leaf on the class tree. Vee is excited for hers to go up next. But cameras give her the BATTYS...so Poppy *paints* her portrait instead!

Can you spot these other kids on the class tree?

When Vee invites Bridget and Poppy over for a sleepover, she doesn't want them to see the GHOSTS, GARGOYLES, **or** GHOULISH pets lurking around the house. Spot these things Vee can use to distract her friends:

laptop

guitar

jack-in-the-box

Justin Teether poster

this doll

playing cards

The Scream Girls have come to stay at the Hauntleys' Scare B&B! While they put on a SHRIEKING good show, find these FANG-TASTIC partygoers:

Day or night, the Hauntleys' home is brimming with SPOOK-TACULAR sights!

Look through Vee's photos to find these ones:

Wonderfully wild Wolfie

Vee's peculiar potion

Gregoria slipping to sleep

Penelope snacking on sweets

Boris in a bind

Chef Remy Bones flipping flapjacks

You can't spell BOO! without the letter B. Bustle back to Vee's living room and find these basic belongings that begin with B:

backpack
bat
bone
book
broom
bucket

Vee's new house is a SHOCK off the old block! Return to Vee's street and look for things that rhyme with these words:

suitor (scooter)
royal (gargoyle)
digit (Bridget)
walk (chalk)
bat (cat)

Scoot back to Vee's school and find items in these colors:

purple
yellow
green
pink
orange
blue

With a little practice, human school is as easy as 1-2-3! Before the bell rings, hurry back to class and count these school supplies:

1 tissue box
2 wall drawings
3 pencils
4 pens
5 paintbrushes

Vee's class tree is made up of many faces—and shapes! Climb back and find these:

square
circle
triangle
diamond
rectangle
star

Vee loves the twinkly stars on her batty pajamas! Can you find 12 more stars hidden in Vee's bedroom?

Twist back to the dance party and find these pretty patterns:

Edgar is always on the lookout for a glimpse of something ghoulish. Flap back through the whole book to find this batty shape hidden in each scene: